D0579861

Gibbons, Gail.
Cats /

c1996.
33305220914828
ca   06/28/10

CATS

SILVER TABBY
SHORTHAIR

RED AND WHITE
SHORTHAIR

BY GAIL GIBBONS

Holiday House
New York

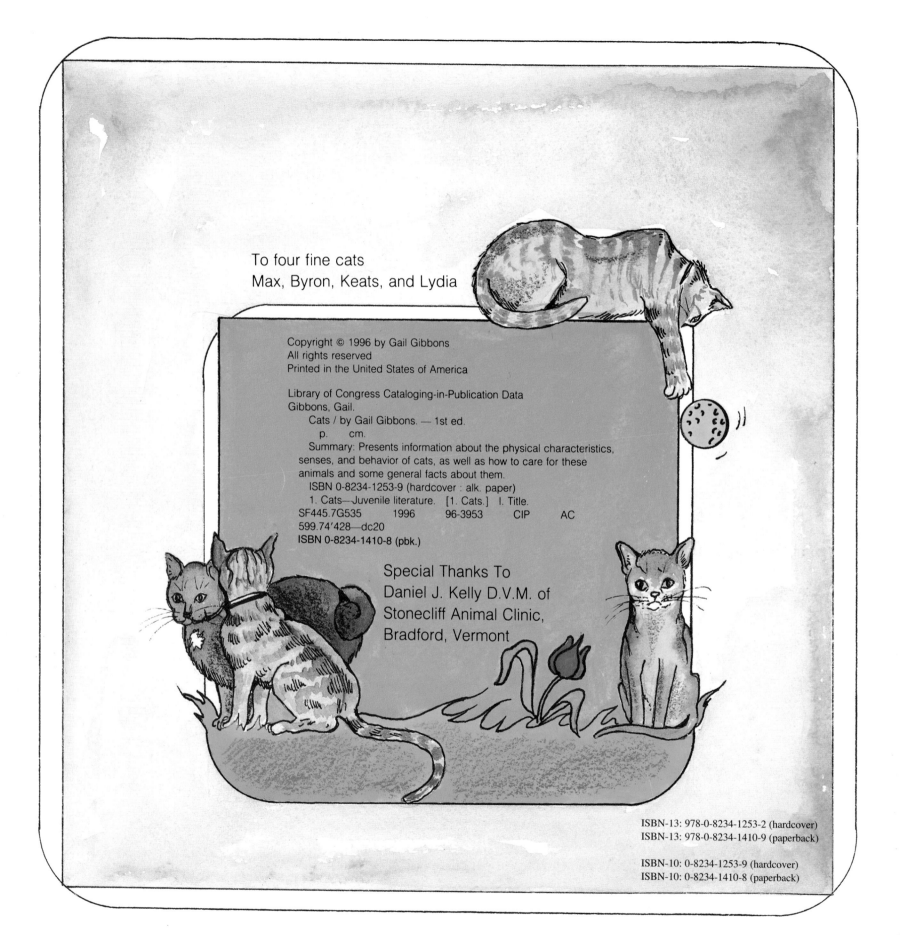

To four fine cats
Max, Byron, Keats, and Lydia

Copyright © 1996 by Gail Gibbons
All rights reserved
Printed in the United States of America

Library of Congress Cataloging-in-Publication Data
Gibbons, Gail.
    Cats / by Gail Gibbons. — 1st ed.
        p.   cm.
    Summary: Presents information about the physical characteristics,
senses, and behavior of cats, as well as how to care for these
animals and some general facts about them.
    ISBN 0-8234-1253-9 (hardcover : alk. paper)
    1. Cats—Juvenile literature. [1. Cats.] I. Title.
SF445.7G535   1996   96-3953   CIP   AC
599.74'428—dc20
ISBN 0-8234-1410-8 (pbk.)

Special Thanks To
Daniel J. Kelly D.V.M. of
Stonecliff Animal Clinic,
Bradford, Vermont

ISBN-13: 978-0-8234-1253-2 (hardcover)
ISBN-13: 978-0-8234-1410-9 (paperback)

ISBN-10: 0-8234-1253-9 (hardcover)
ISBN-10: 0-8234-1410-8 (paperback)

Cats can be good pets. It's fun to watch them play, pet their soft sleek fur or curl up next to one while reading a book. Cats can be faithful and loving friends.

AFRICAN WILDCAT

SEAL POINT SIAMESE

BLACK SHORTHAIR

BROWN TABBY SHORTHAIR

All cats belong to the cat family called Felidae. Cats are felines. They have been around for a long time. Their first ancestors lived about 55 million years ago. Today's domestic cats are descendants of the African wildcats that were excellent hunters.

RED ABYSSINIAN

Egyptians probably were the first people to tame cats about 4000 years ago. Because cats are such good hunters, those people used them to catch mice and rats where grain was stored. Those cats were prized pets.

These are PUREBRED cats.

SHORTHAIR BREED

CHOCOLATE POINT SIAMESE

LONGHAIR BREED

BLUE LONGHAIR

There are big cats and small cats. Some have small pointy faces. Others have big furry heads. That's because there are different breeds of cats. There are two main groups of breeds, the longhair and the shorthair.

MIXED BREEDS

Cats that have been carefully bred for the way they look are purebred cats. Most pet cats are mixed breeds that come from a mixture of two or more breeds. All these cats make good pets.

Almost all cats have the same basic characteristics.

SILVER TABBY SHORTHAIR

INCISORS

CANINE
TEETH
or
FANGS

JAW

MOLARS

Cats have thirty teeth that are designed for hunting. Their four big sharp teeth called canine teeth, or fangs, are used for tearing food. Their small front teeth are called incisors and are used for biting. They use their back molars to grind and crush food into tiny pieces before swallowing it.

Cats are wonderful hunters because of their strong and powerful legs, sharp claws and flexible bodies. They can move quickly, jump and climb. Cats don't use their entire feet like people do. They don't stand on their heels. They have pads on the bottoms of their paws.

CREAM AND WHITE SHORTHAIR

TOES

TOES

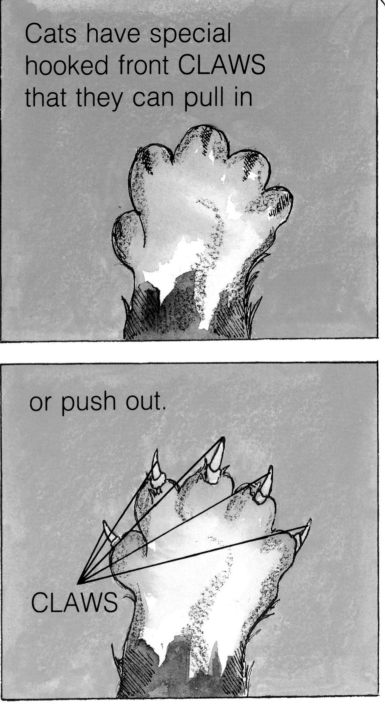

Cats have special hooked front CLAWS that they can pull in

or push out.

CLAWS

Cats have five toes on each front paw and four toes on each hind paw. These toes have claws that are used for grabbing and holding. They keep their claws very sharp by scratching against trees and other objects.

They have excellent sight. At night cats can see six times better than people. This is because cats have a special layer of cells at the back of their eyes that reflect more light when their pupils enlarge. During the bright daylight hours, their pupils narrow to slits that let less light inside.

EAR

RUDDY ABYSSINIAN

Hearing is a cat's second most important sense. Cats can hear many high pitched sounds that most people can't hear. They turn their cupped ears to pick up any surrounding sounds.

BLACK AND WHITE SHORTHAIR

NOSE

Cats have a keen sense of smell, too. Inside their noses are about 70 million scent cells that help identify odors. They also have an unusual way of detecting smells by using a part inside their mouth called Jacobson's organ. This area is sensitive to taste, too.

WHISKERS

RED TABBY SHORTHAIR

They have an excellent sense of touch. Often, cats use their paws and noses for touching. They also have many whiskers that grow in rows at the sides of their mouths, above their eyes and on the insides of their front legs. These whiskers are attached to many nerves, which are sensitive to touch.

"MEOW . . ." "HISSSSS . . ." Cats make many sounds that mean different things. A "MEOW" can mean they want to be noticed. A "HISSSSS . . ." or a growl means they're angry. Sometimes cats "YOWL" when they are upset.

PURRR . . .

AMERICAN WIREHAIR

Scientists believe cats "PURRR" by using two sets of vocal cords, one above the other, in their throats. Often, cats "PURRR . . ." when they are content.

Cats communicate in other ways, too. A happy cat's ears move forward and its tail is held high. An angry cat lays its ears back, its pupils become slits, the hair on its back stands up and its tail bushes out. A frightened cat's ears go flat on its head and the pupils of its eyes become round.

Another way cats communicate is by using scent glands at the base of their tails and at their cheeks and temples. They do this by rubbing their scent to mark their territory. Only cats can smell this scent. Often cats that live together rub each other's heads together to show affection and leave their scents on each other. Often cats rub up against people's legs to say, "You are mine."

BROWN TABBY SHORTHAIR

Cats have two layers of fur, the outer fur and the under fur which is soft and fluffy. They use their rough tongues to lick their fur clean. They use their teeth to smooth matted and tangled fur.

RED MACKEREL TABBY

Cats love to sleep, sometimes as much as sixteen hours a day. They don't usually sleep for long periods of time. Instead they sleep for short periods. That's where the phrase "cat nap" comes from. Often they choose strange places to nap.

They spend most of their time playing and exploring. Kittens will make good pets if they spend time around people at this time. Kittens are fuzzy and cute.

ANIMAL SHELTER

RED TABBY SHORTHAIR

When a kitten is about eight weeks old, it is old enough to leave its mother. Some people like to adopt kittens, and some people like to adopt older cats.

CARING FOR YOUR KITTEN

Handle your kitten gently and speak softly. If you play roughly with your kitten it may become an aggressive cat.

Feed your kitten three small meals a day. At first feed it canned or dry kitten food. Later, when it's older, it will be able to eat regular canned or dry cat food.

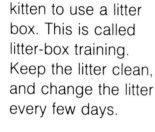

Patiently teach your kitten to use a litter box. This is called litter-box training. Keep the litter clean, and change the litter every few days.

Your kitten should have fresh water available at all times.

Make sure your kitten has safe toys to play with. All kittens need exercise.

Don't leave your kitten alone outside.

A kitten loves to scratch its front claws on things like curtains and furniture. Train it to use its own scratching post.

Make your kitten a nice, cozy bed to sleep in.

Take your kitten to the veterinarian for its checkup and kitten shots.

Unfortunately, there are many unwanted kittens in our world. If you don't want your kitten to have kittens when it's older, it should be neutered if it's male or spayed if it's female. This should be done by a vet.

Remember . . . your kitten needs love and care just like you do.

CARING FOR YOUR CAT

Feed your cat at least once a day. A meal may be canned or dry cat food, or both.

Cats love to scratch with their front claws. Train your cat to use its own scratching post.

Your cat needs a litter box when it's inside. Keep the litter clean.

Your cat should have a nice, cozy bed.

Your cat should have fresh water available at all times.

Take your cat to the veterinarian for its yearly checkup and shots. If your cat looks sick or injured, bring it to a vet.

Your cat should have safe toys to play with.

If you don't want your cat to have kittens, it should be neutered if it's male or spayed if it's female. This should be done by a vet.

Make sure your cat has a safe place to play outside.

Most of all, your cat needs you. Love your cat!

SEAL POINT
BIRMAN

BEST

Often, people enter their cats in cat shows. The cat that is judged best is the champion. The first cat show in the United States was held about 1870. Today there are 300 cat clubs in North America.

TORTOISESHELL
SHORTHAIR

BLACK SHORTHAIR

Kittens and cats are so much fun to play with . . . but, best of all,
they are wonderful pets.

CATS IN HISTORY

About 4000 years ago, the ancient Egyptians carved figures of cats. They worshiped cats as gods.

Phoenician traders probably brought cats to Europe aboard their ships about 1100 years ago.

The cat was a symbol of liberty in ancient Rome.

European traders, explorers and colonists brought domestic cats to the Americas during the 1700s. These domestic cats became the ancestors of most of the cats that live in the United States today.

SOME PEOPLE BELIEVE . . .

Some people think black cats are evil and unlucky. Others claim black cats bring them good luck.

Many sailors bring a cat aboard for good luck.

Some people think cats with extra toes bring good luck.

SOME PEOPLE SAY . . .

"Curiosity killed the cat." This means a person who is very curious can get into trouble.

"Playing cat and mouse." This means someone is teasing or being coy with someone else.

"When the cat's away, the mice will play!" This means someone may get into mischief when no one is there to watch.

"The cat's meow." This means someone or something is the very best.

MEOW . . .

A cat usually lives to be eight to sixteen years old.

When a cat or kitten tumbles from a high place, messages from its inner ears to the brain tell the cat how to land. It gains its balance to flip over and land on its paws.

Often cat owners put flea collars on their pets so they won't get fleas.

It is believed that the world's biggest cat was Himmy, a tabby that lived in Australia. It weighed 45 pounds!

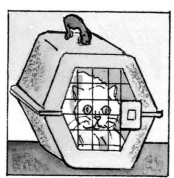

When a cat owner goes to the veterinarian or takes a cat on a trip, the cat should travel in a cat carrier or a ventilated box so it can't escape.

The world's champion mouse catcher was Towser. It's believed she caught 23,000 mice during her lifetime.

Each cat's nose covering is different from any other cat's. Its nose print is unique, just like a person's fingerprint is unique.

There have been many famous stories written about cats. Two of them are "PUSS 'N BOOTS" and "THE OWL AND THE PUSSYCAT".